Wizard Wig

First published in 2008
by Wayland

This paperback edition published in 2009

Text copyright © Anne Cassidy 2008
Illustration copyright © Martin Remphry 2008

Wayland
338 Euston Road
London NW1 3BH

Wayland Australia
Hachette Children's Books
Level 17/207 Kent Street
Sydney, NSW 2000

Series Editor: Louise John
Cover design: Paul Cherrill
Design: D.R.ink
Consultant: Shirley Bickler

A CIP catalogue record for this book is available from the British Library.

ISBN 9780750251891 (hbk)
ISBN 9780750251907 (pbk)

Printed in China

Wayland is a division of Hachette Children's Books,
an Hachette Livre UK Company

www.hachettelivre.co.uk

Wizard Wig

Written by Anne Cassidy
Illustrated by Martin Remphry

WAYLAND

Wizzle the wizard was casting a spell.

"I command you to become a magic mirror!"

"Whoever looks into this mirror will be beautiful!" Wizzle said.
The queen looked into the mirror.

"No!" cried out Wizzle's sister, Wanda.

But it was too late. Wizzle's spell
had gone badly wrong – again!
The queen began to sob.

Later, the king came to
Wizzle's room.

"Where is my wizard?" he shouted.

"Look," the king cried, "I'm losing my hair – it's all falling out. Soon I'll have no hair left!"

"I have a spell which makes hair grow," said Wizzle.

Wanda took an old spell book from the shelf.

"Get me a unicorn's horn, some fairy wings and... a dragon's egg! That should do it," said Wizzle, and he mixed everything together.

Wizzle put the mixture onto the king's head.

He whispered some magic words.
"Izzle, Wizzle, Woo!"

The king's head fizzed and sparkled.
His hair began to grow longer,
thicker and fluffier. He even had
curls and ringlets!

It grew so much that it reached
the floor.
"Make it stop," the king cried.
"Stop it at once!"

Wizzle didn't know what to do!
He didn't know how to stop it.

He picked up a jug of water and
threw it over the king's head.

The king's hair fell out.
He was completely bald!

The king was furious. His face
turned red. He shook his fist.

"You are the worst wizard in the
world. Get out of my castle!"

Wizard Wizzle left the castle.
He felt very sad.

"Don't worry," Wanda shouted, "I'll think of a way to get you back in the castle."

Inside the castle, Wanda saw a servant weaving.

She was making a beautiful piece of cloth.

Wanda had an idea. She told the servant what she wanted to do.

The servant smiled.

That night Wanda crept into the king's bedroom, while he was asleep.

She measured his head with a
tape measure.

The next morning, Wizzle came
to see the king.

"Please give me one more chance!"
he said. "I have found the best spell
ever to make new hair."

"I have hair from a lion's mane, some feathers from a golden eagle and some diamond dust."

Wizzle sprinkled them over a box.

"Izzle, Wizle, Woo! The king must have beautiful hair!" he whispered.

Wanda lifted the lid. Inside there was a wig.

"This is fantastic," said the king.
"I really love it!"

"Maybe you're not such a bad wizard after all," he said, smiling at Wizzle.

START READING is a series of highly enjoyable books for beginner readers. They have been carefully graded to match the Book Bands widely used in schools. This enables readers to be sure they choose books that match their own reading ability.

The Bands are:

Pink / Band 1
Red / Band 2
Yellow / Band 3
Blue / Band 4
Green / Band 5
Orange / Band 6
Turquoise / Band 7
Purple / Band 8
Gold / Band 9

START READING books can be read independently or shared with an adult. They promote the enjoyment of reading through satisfying stories supported by fun illustrations.

Anne Cassidy has written lots of books for children. Many of them are about talking animals who get into trouble. She has two dogs, Charlie and Dave, but, sadly, neither of them talk to her! This time she wanted to write about a funny wizard who gets his spells mixed up.

Martin Remphry grew up on the tiny Channel Island of Sark. He has always loved drawing, especially spooky things such as witches and wizards, so it was a dream come true for him to illustrate Wizzle. He loves the funny ingredients Wizzle uses for his spells, even if they don't always work as he hopes!